Enid Blyton's

Goodnight
STORIES

For further information on Enid Blyton please contact www.blyton.com

ISBN 1-84135-030-3

First published 2000 by Award Publications Limited,
3rd impression 2003

Published by Award Publications Limited
1st Floor, 27 Longford Street, London NW1 3DZ

Printed in Singapore

Enid Blyton's

Goodnight
STORIES

AWARD PUBLICATIONS LIMITED

The Stories

1
The Land of Blue Mountains

2
The Enchanted Slippers

3
Jumbo Saves the Day

1

The Land
of Blue Mountains

Illustrated by Maggie Downer

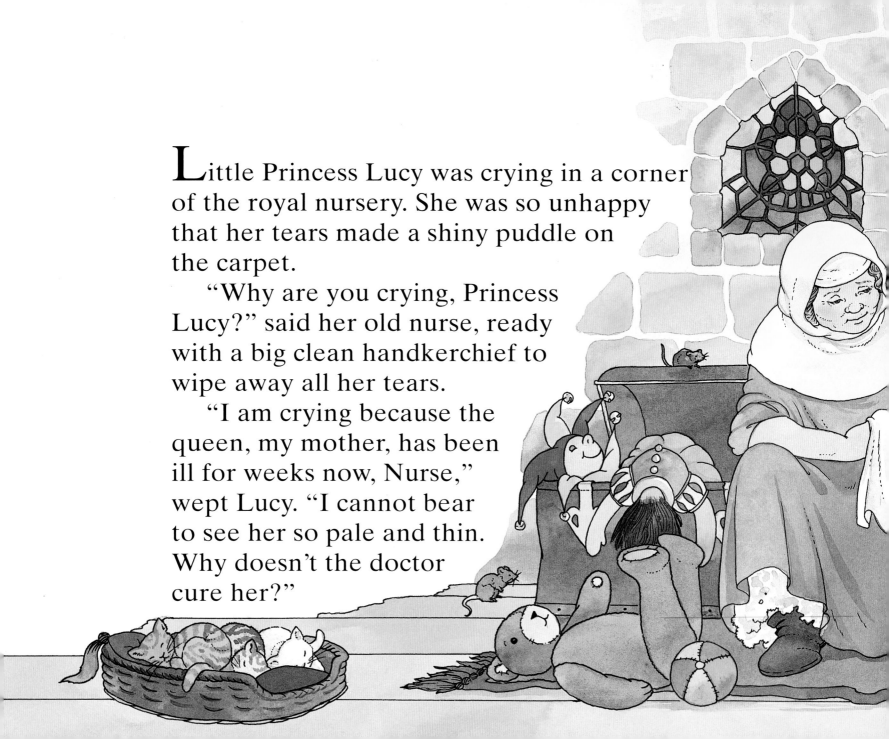

Little Princess Lucy was crying in a corner of the royal nursery. She was so unhappy that her tears made a shiny puddle on the carpet.

"Why are you crying, Princess Lucy?" said her old nurse, ready with a big clean handkerchief to wipe away all her tears.

"I am crying because the queen, my mother, has been ill for weeks now, Nurse," wept Lucy. "I cannot bear to see her so pale and thin. Why doesn't the doctor cure her?"

"Her illness cannot be cured by a doctor," said the old nurse, sadly. "A spell has been cast upon her, a spell that was cast before my very eyes!"

"Tell me what you saw," said Lucy who was now weeping faster than ever.

"I saw a little man from the Land of Blue Mountains," said the nurse. "He passed me as I lit the lamp outside your mother's bedroom. He slipped into her room and asked her for her wonderful jade necklace.

"She would not give it to him so, before he left, he muttered some magic words. It was a spell I am sure! The next day she fell ill, and has never left her bed since."

"Oh, Nurse!" said Princess Lucy, in dismay. "Why should he put a spell on my mother?"

"The jade necklace came from that mysterious land," said the nurse. "And it is said that the little man who sold it to your father, the king, has always longed for it back."

"If only my father was home!" sighed Lucy. "But he is far away, exploring new lands. Who else can help my mother, Nurse?"

"No one," said the nurse. "None would dare to go to the Blue Mountains save your father."

"Where is the Land of Blue Mountains?" asked Lucy. "Tell me."

"Come with me, and I will show you," said the nurse. So Lucy followed her up hundreds of stairs until she reached the highest room in the palace. It was a little round room with one tiny round window set in the western wall.

"Look through that window," said the nurse. "It is the only window in the palace that looks upon that strange land."

Lucy saw a glorious sight. Far away rose peak upon peak of deep-blue mountains, their summits tipped with gold in the setting sun. White clouds floated round the blue mountainsides, and the valleys between were dark purple.

It was so strange and wonderful that Lucy longed to go there. She looked for a long time until her nurse grew tired of waiting, and told her it was time for bed.

"If I went there I might find the little man who put the spell on my mother," she thought as she climbed into bed but when she asked how to get there, her nurse said,

"Nobody knows but your father. It is a cold, stony land, and the people there have hearts as cold and stony as their mountains. Now go to sleep, Lucy, and forget all you have seen."

But in her dreams Lucy dreamt that she was following a little humpbacked man up a blue mountainside, calling to him to stop. She dreamed that she came to a well, full of gleaming, golden water. And last of all she dreamed that her mother was well again.

When she woke up, the dawn was just creeping in from the eastern sky. Lucy put on her bedroom slippers and ran up to the highest room in the palace. Once more she peeped through the round window and saw the gleaming blue mountains.

But how strange! They seemed much nearer than the night before, and a broad road ran to them from the edge of the palace gardens.

In a trice Lucy had made up her mind. She would go to the Blue Mountains herself. Quickly she ran to her room and dressed. Then she went downstairs and opened the garden gate. There lay the road, gleaming like gold in the morning sun. She stepped out on to it, and as she did so, she heard a bark behind her.

It was Saxon, her dog. He had heard her footsteps and had come to join her. Lucy was so pleased to see him.

"Oh, Saxon," she said. "Will you come with me to the Land of Blue Mountains?"

Saxon licked her hand, and then knelt down beside her. He wanted her to climb on to his broad back, for he often gave the little Princess a ride.

"Oh, that is a splendid idea!" cried Lucy. "Now we shall soon be there!" So off they went down the gleaming golden road, with the tall blue mountains shining far away in front of them, and the palace slowly growing smaller and smaller behind them.

After some time they came to a clear stream at the roadside, and they both drank from it. Then suddenly the dog gave a loud bark and pointed with his paw to the road behind them.

Lucy looked – and what a strange sight she saw. The road was disappearing!

"Oh, the road is going!" she cried to Saxon. "Quick! We must reach the Land of Blue Mountains before the road is quite gone!"

Off they raced, while behind them the road gradually disappeared as if someone were rolling it up. Great rocks and thick woods sprang up where the road had been. Faster and faster galloped the panting dog, and nearer and nearer came the mountains.

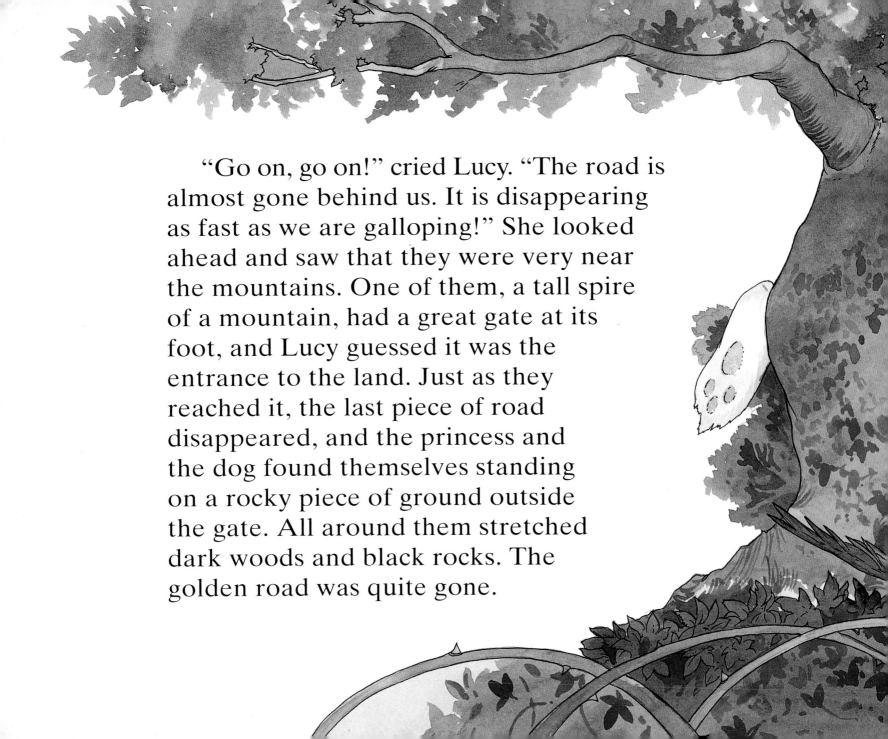

"Go on, go on!" cried Lucy. "The road is almost gone behind us. It is disappearing as fast as we are galloping!" She looked ahead and saw that they were very near the mountains. One of them, a tall spire of a mountain, had a great gate at its foot, and Lucy guessed it was the entrance to the land. Just as they reached it, the last piece of road disappeared, and the princess and the dog found themselves standing on a rocky piece of ground outside the gate. All around them stretched dark woods and black rocks. The golden road was quite gone.

The gate swung open and they passed through together. Blue mountains towered up on every side. Their sides were bare and stony, and as blue as forget-me-nots. The little streams that fell down the sides were blue too, and the only plants that grew there were great bright blue things as large as saucers.

"What a strange country!" whispered Lucy and Saxon licked her hand gently to stop her from feeling afraid.

They chose one of the paths that led between the mountains and followed it. Lucy was surprised to see no one about – but at last she spied two little figures, and she called to them. They stopped and looked at her in astonishment.

As she drew near she saw that they were dressed in blue wool, and had woollen caps on their heads. Their eyes were cold and blue, and Lucy did not like them.

"What are you doing here?" the little folk demanded. "Aren't you cold without a coat?"

"Not at all!" said Lucy, in surprise. "The sun is very warm. You must be hot in all those clothes."

"Only those with warm hearts can keep warm here," said one of the little men. "We folk of the Blue Mountains are cold, even on the hottest day. Why did you come here?"

"I came to find the little man who put a spell on my mother," said Lucy. "He once sold a jade necklace to my father, the king."

"That must be Blizzard, who lives at the top of this path," said the little folk. "But be careful of him. He is the coldest one of all."

Lucy said goodbye and took the narrow path they pointed out to her which led up the steep mountainside.

"I am so hot I don't know what to do," said Lucy after a while. "However can these people here be

cold when they have all these
mountains to climb!"
    Just then a little humpbacked
man came toiling up another
path nearby. Lucy called to
him, but his sheepskin cap
was pulled so firmly
over his ears that he
did not hear her.
    "Perhaps that is
Blizzard," she said
to Saxon. "Come
on. We'll
follow him."

So on they went following the little blue man up the great blue mountainside. At last he went inside a small cottage set into the hillside. Lucy and Saxon followed, and knocked loudly.

Blizzard came to the door in surprise. Not many visitors came to his cottage.

"What do you want?" he asked.

"I am Princess Lucy and I have come to ask you to lift the spell from my mother," said Lucy. "You have made her ill, and I want her well again."

Blizzard's eyes were like two shining sapphires.

"You have come to this cold, stony country," he said, "where we all shiver and freeze, and yet you have no coat and no hat. Let me feel your hand. Why, it is warm as fire!"

"And yours is as cold as ice," said Princess Lucy with a shiver.

"It is cold as my heart," said Blizzard mournfully. "All people with cold hearts are sent to live here, and we never feel warm. If only I had a warm heart like yours! How happy I should be!"

"Yes and you would be kind too," said Lucy. "It was cruel of you to put a spell on my poor mother. Tell me how to undo it."

"Why should I?" said Blizzard, his little cold eyes gleaming like ice. "You have nothing to give me in exchange."

Lucy began to cry. Her tears fell down her cheeks, and Blizzard touched them in wonder.

"Why, even your tears are warm," he said.

"I would give anything to have a heart as warm as yours!"

"Then take that horrid spell off my mother and I will give you my warm heart and take your cold one!" said the little princess, bravely.

Blizzard could not believe his ears at first, but as soon as he knew that Lucy meant what she said he took her by the hand and hurried her down the mountainside.

"We will go to the well of golden water," he said. "A bottle of that will cure your mother. Then we will go the Ice Maiden who lives at the top of the highest mountain and she will change our hearts for us. Oh, I shall be so happy when I get your warm heart for my own!"

Lucy hurried after him. On and on they went, until they came at last to the foot of a towering blue mountain, the highest of all, and at the very top was a shimmering palace of blue ice. They started up the winding path that led to the top and had not been climbing long before they came to a well, the same one that Lucy had seen in her dream. She looked down and saw golden water at the bottom. There was no bucket to send down, and Lucy wondered how they were to get the magic water. But the little man soon showed her.

He tied a rope round himself, knotted one end to a post of the well, and then let himself down to the water. He filled a bottle, and then, with Lucy's help, pulled himself up again. Where his clothes

had touched the water he shone like the sunset.
He gave the bottle to Lucy, who slipped it into
her pocket.

Lucy felt a tug at her dress, and saw Saxon looking at her. He wanted her to climb on his back and run away without giving her warm heart to the little blue man. But she would not.

"No, Saxon," she whispered in his ear. "A princess cannot break her promise."

On they went to the shimmering blue palace and passed through a gate of blue sapphire so beautiful that it hurt Lucy's eyes to look at it. Then into a great hall they went, and the little princess saw a giantess sitting on a throne of silver.

"What do you want?" asked the Ice Maiden, and her voice sounded like ice cracking on a pond.

"This princess is going to give me her warm heart in exchange for my cold one," said Blizzard.

"Will you make the magic that will change our hearts?"

"Why do you want a warm heart?" asked the Ice Maiden. "Warm hearts are a nuisance. They make their owners do kind and unselfish deeds. It is much nicer to be cold and selfish."

"But her tears are warm!" cried Blizzard. "It must be wonderful to have warm tears and a warm heart to match!"

The giantess laughed, and it was like a shower of hail falling on a glass roof.

"If you wish it, I will change your hearts," she said. "You must hold hands and walk together to the gateway of our land. Kiss her twice when you get there, and look deep into her eyes. Then you will have her heart and she will have yours."

"Thank you," said Blizzard, and they left the palace, with Saxon following behind. Down the mountainside they went, holding hands, and as they went Lucy's hand became cold, and Blizzard's became warm.

For a long time they walked, until at last they reached the gate through which the princess and her dog had passed that very morning. It was dusk now, and the moon was rising. For a minute it went behind a dark cloud. Blizzard let go of Lucy's hand, and waited for the moon to come out again. But before it did so, he felt two kisses, and found himself looking into two eyes, while two hands rested on his shoulders.

Suddenly there came a pain in his heart and it became warm. Blizzard felt so glad that the tears poured down his cheeks and he could not see.

"My heart is warm, my heart is warm!" he cried. "I shall never be cold again! I am happy, happy, happy!"

He slipped through the gates and ran back to the Land of Blue Mountains, leaving Lucy standing alone very much astonished.

"But how can your heart be warm?" she called. "You didn't kiss me, nor look into my eyes! My heart is not cold. It is as warm as ever."

But there was no answer. Blizzard had gone.

Then Lucy felt a wet nose against her arm, and guessed what had happened. Saxon had pretended to be her, when the moon had gone behind that dark cloud! He had stood up in front of Blizzard with his paws on the little man's shoulders, and had licked him twice!

"Oh, dear, kind Saxon, you have given up your own warm heart in place of mine!" cried Lucy, hugging him. "I think you are the most wonderful dog in the world! But what has happened to Blizzard's cold heart? Have *you* got it?"

Saxon mournfully nodded his head. Then, very sadly he trotted down the road beside the princess. His heart was heavy and cold, and he felt strange and unhappy. But he also felt glad because he had saved Lucy's warm heart for her, and she had the bottle of golden water safe.

The road spread out in front of them once more and they set off towards the moonlit palace, shining in the distance. It was dawn by the time they arrived and Lucy ran through the sleeping rooms to her mother's bedside. She poured the golden water into a glass and gave it to her mother to drink.

The queen sat up with a cry.

"The spell is gone!" she said. "I am better! Oh, Lucy, tell me where you got the golden water from!"

Lucy told her story, and at the end the queen cried to think of poor Saxon and his cold heart.

"See him sitting by the fire, shivering," said Lucy. "What can we do for him, Mother?" Just then the old nurse came into the room and cried out in delight to see Lucy, and to find the queen better once more. When she heard about the poor dog, she smiled.

"Don't fret," she said. "His heart will soon be better. No dog can possess a cold heart for long. Feed him on milk mixed with your tears for him, and his heart will be as warm as ever in a few days!"

And so his heart gradually became warmer, and his bark became happier and happier, until at last his heart was as warm as ever. The Princess Lucy was so grateful that she had a fine collar made for him, and from it she hung a tiny golden heart. He will show it to you if ever you see him!

2

The Enchanted
Slippers

Illustrated by Maggie Downer

Once upon a time there was a boy called
William, who lived with his mother at the foot of
some high hills. Nobody lived up on the hills for it
was said that dwarfs lived in caves there, and no
one liked to walk on the sunny hillside.

William's mother often warned him not to go wandering in the hills, and to beware of any strange thing that he saw for fear it was enchanted. But William saw nothing at all, and he wasn't a bit afraid of dwarfs, no, nor giants either. Not he!

One day he went to look for wild strawberries at the foot of the hills. They were hard to find but, just as he was about to give up, he suddenly saw a sunny bank, just a little way up the hill, where he was quite certain he would find some.

To get there he had to cross a very boggy piece of ground – and dear me, before he knew what was happening he was sinking right down in it!

Quickly, William slipped off his heavy boots, which were held tightly in the mud, and leapt lightly to a dry tuft of grass.

"Bother!" he cried, "I've lost my boots! I shall get thorns and prickles in my feet if I'm not careful."

Then he saw a strange sight – for on a dry flat stone just in front of him there was a pair of fine red slippers with silver buckles! William stared at them in surprise. Who could they belong to? He looked around but he couldn't see anyone.

"Hello! Is anybody about?" William shouted loudly. "Whose shoes are these?" But there was no answer at all.

William looked at the shoes again. It seemed a pity not to borrow them when he had none. He wouldn't spoil them – he would just wear them home and then try to find out who the owner was.

So he picked up the shoes and slipped them on his feet. They fitted him exactly.

William thought they looked very nice. He stood up and tried them. Yes, they really might have been made for him!

"I'd better go back down the hill," he thought, suddenly. "I've come too far up, and mother always warns me not to."

He turned to go back down – but to his surprise his feet walked the other way! Yes, they walked *up* the hill, instead of down!

William couldn't believe it. Here he was trying to walk down the hill and he couldn't. He tried to force his feet to turn round but it was no good at all! They simply wouldn't!

"Oh no!" said William. "Why did I meddle with these shoes? I might have guessed they were magic! I've got to go where the shoes lead me, I suppose. I wonder, though, if I could take them off."

But his feet wouldn't stop walking long enough for him to try, so on he had to go. Up the hill his feet took him, along a steep path, and up to a small yellow door in the hillside.

As he came up to it, the door opened and a little dwarf, dressed in red and yellow, looked out. He grinned when he saw William.

"Ha! So my shoes have caught someone at last. Good!"

"You've no right to lay traps like that," said William, crossly, as his feet took him through the door. "Take these shoes off my feet at once!"

"Oh, no, my fine fellow!" said the dwarf, chuckling. "Now I've got you, I'm going to keep you. It's no good trying to get those shoes off – they're stuck on by magic, and only magic will get them off!"

"Well, what are you going to do with me?" asked William.

"I want an errand-boy," said the dwarf. "I do lots of business with witches, wizards and giants, sending out all sorts of spells and charms – and I want someone to deliver them for me."

"I don't see why I should work for you!" said William. "I want to go home."

"How dare you talk to me like that!" cried the dwarf, flying into a rage. "I'll turn you into a frog!"

"All right, all right!" said William, with a sigh. "But I shall escape as soon as I possibly can."

"Not as long as you've got those shoes on," said the dwarf, with a grin. "They will always bring you back to me, no matter where you go!"

Poor William. He had to start on his new job straight away!

The dwarf wrapped up a strange little blue flower in a piece of yellow paper and told William to take it to Witch Twiddle. The shoes started off at once and, puffing and panting, William climbed right to the top of the hill where he found a small cottage, half tumbling down. Green smoke came from the chimney and from inside came a high, chanting voice. It was the witch singing a spell.

"Come in!" she called when William knocked at the door. He went inside and found Witch Twiddle stirring a big black pot over a small fire. She was singing strings of magic words, and William stood open-mouthed, watching.

"What are you gaping at, nincompoop?" said the witch, impatiently.

"I'm not a nincompoop!" exclaimed William. "It's just that I've never seen boiling water send up green steam before!"

"Then you *are* a nincompoop!" said the witch. "What have you come here for anyway?"

"I've come from the dwarf down the hill," said William. "He sent you this."

He held out the little yellow package, and the witch pounced on it greedily.

"Ha! The spell he said he would give me! Good!" William wanted to sit down and have a rest, but the enchanted slippers walked him out of the cottage and down the hill again.

Trimble the Dwarf was waiting for him with a heap of small packages to deliver.

"Look here!" said William, firmly, "I'm not going to take all those. I want a rest."

"Well, you'll have to do without one," said the dwarf. "I want these packages delivered. This goes to Castaspell the Wizard, and this to Dwindle the Dwarf, and this to Rumble the Giant."

"But I don't know where they live," said William.

"That doesn't matter," said Trimble. "The enchanted slippers will take you there!"

And so they did. It was most peculiar. First they took him to a little wood, in the middle of which was a very high tower with no door. A neat little notice said "Castaspell the Wizard."

"That's funny," said William looking
all round. "There's no way to get in!"
He knocked on the wall of the tower.
"Come in, come in!" cried a voice.
"How?" asked William. "There's
no door."
"Oh, bless me if I haven't
forgotten to put the door back
again!" said a grumbling voice
from inside. "Come back, door!"
At once a bright-green door
appeared in the tower.

William stared at it, astonished. Then he opened it and stepped into a small, round room where a hunched-up old man sat reading an enormous book. His beard was so long and thick that it spread all over the floor. William had to take care not to tread on it.

"Here you are," said William. "It's a parcel from Trimble the Dwarf."

William gave the old man the package and left. To his surprise the door vanished as soon as he was outside. It was most peculiar.

His enchanted slippers would not let him stay for a moment. They ran him out of the wizard's wood and took him halfway down the other side of the hill before they stopped.

"What's the matter now?" wondered William. "I can't see any house. These slippers have made a mistake. I hope they won't keep me out here in the cold all day!"

Just then the earth began to shake beneath his feet! He felt frightened, and wondered if there was an earthquake. Then suddenly he heard a cross little voice.

"Get off my front door! I can't open it. Get off, I say!"

The voice seemed to come from down below. William felt the earth shaking under him again – and then, to his astonishment he saw that he was standing on a neat brown trapdoor, just the colour of the hillside! On the trapdoor was a little nameplate that said: "Dwindle the Dwarf."

"I'm so sorry!" called William. "I didn't know I was standing on your front door! But my feet won't get off it."

There was an angry noise below. Then suddenly someone pushed the trapdoor open so hard that William was sent flying into the air and fell down with a bump.

"Careful!" shouted William, crossly. "You sent me flying!"

"Serve you right," said the bad-tempered dwarf, sticking his head out of the open trapdoor. "What do you want here, anyway? Are you the boy that brings the potatoes?"

"No, I am *not*!" said William. "I've been sent by Trimble the Dwarf to bring you this package."

The dwarf snatched the parcel from his hand and disappeared down the trapdoor at once slamming it shut behind him.

"Go away," he called. "And don't you ever stand on my door again."

At once William's enchanted slippers took him back up the hill at a fast trot.

"I've only got to go to Giant Rumble now," said William. "Thank goodness! I feel quite exhausted!"

Soon he came to something that looked like a big golden pole. As he got near it he saw that it was a long, long ladder of gold, reaching up into the sky and into a large black cloud.

His feet began to climb up the ladder, and dear me, it was very hard work! Before he was very far up he badly wanted a rest – but the enchanted slippers wouldn't stop. Up and up they went!

After a long while William reached the top. He looked round

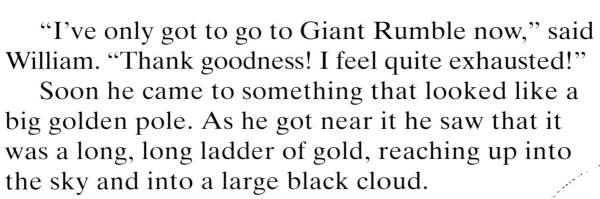

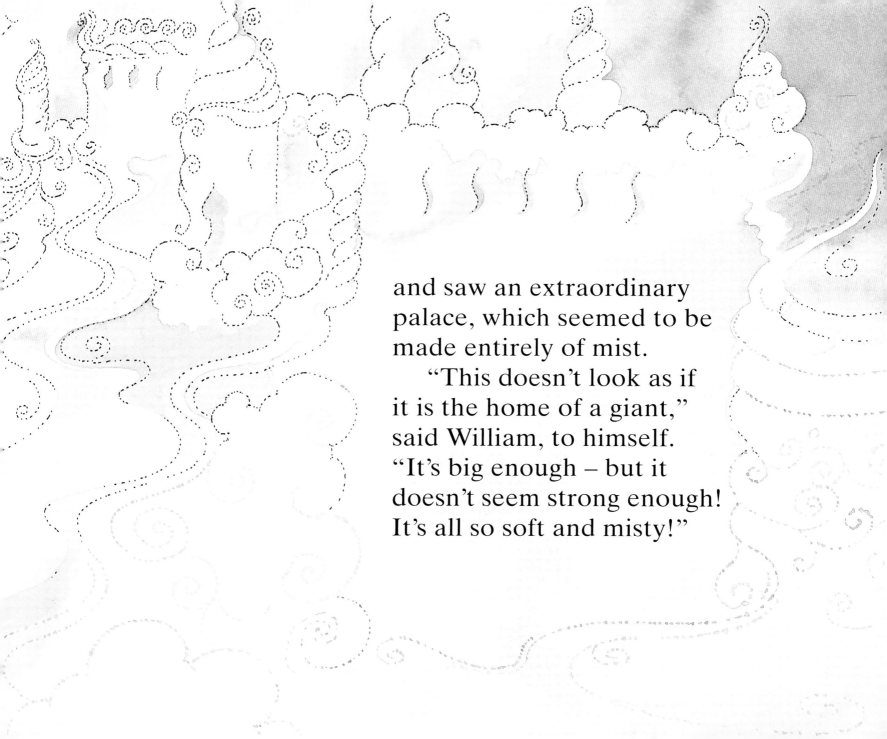

and saw an extraordinary palace, which seemed to be made entirely of mist.

"This doesn't look as if it is the home of a giant," said William, to himself. "It's big enough – but it doesn't seem strong enough! It's all so soft and misty!"

But all the same, a giant *did* live there. The front door opened as William drew near, and inside he saw a great hall, higher than the highest tree he had ever seen. Sitting at a carved table was a giant with a broad, kindly face. He looked down smilingly at the boy as he walked forward.

"Where do you come from, boy?" he asked.

"From Trimble the Dwarf," answered William. "He sent you this parcel."

"About time too," said the giant, stretching out such an enormous hand for it that William felt quite frightened. "Don't be afraid, my boy. I won't hurt you. I'm a cloud-giant, and I live up here to make the thunder you hear sometimes. But I do no harm to anyone."

The giant opened the parcel and then frowned angrily. "The dwarf has sent me the wrong spell again!" he grumbled. "Do *you* know anything about spells, boy?"

"Nothing at all," said William.

"Dear me, that's a pity," said Rumble. "I'm doing a summer-thunder spell, and I've got to multiply twelve lightning flashes by eleven thunder claps. I don't know the answer. Trimble said he'd send it to me, but he hasn't, I'm sure."

"What does he say the answer is?" asked William, who knew his tables very well indeed.

"He says that twelve flashes of lightning multiplied by eleven claps of thunder make ninety-nine storm-clouds," said Rumble.

"Quite wrong," said William. "Twelve times eleven is one hundred and thirty-two."

"Well, is that so?" said the giant. "I *am* pleased! Now I can do my spell. I'm really very much obliged to you. I suppose I can't possibly do anything for you in return?"

"Well, yes, you can," said William, at once. "You can tell me how to get rid of these slippers."

"Well, the only way to get rid of them is to put them on someone else," said Rumble. "Tell me who you'd like to put them on and I'll tell you how to get them off!"

"I'd like to make that horrid little Dwarf Trimble wear them, and send him off to the moon!" said William.

"Ha, ha, ha, ha!" laughed the giant. "Best joke I've heard for years! That would serve him right. Now listen. Wait till the dwarf is asleep, and then slip these tiny stones into your slippers. You will find that they come off at once. Put them on Trimble's feet before you can count ten, and tell him where to go. He'll go all right! The slippers will start him walking and he'll never come back."

"Oh thank you," said William gratefully and took the small pebbles that Rumble gave him. He said goodbye to the kindly giant and then climbed quickly down the ladder.

He was soon back at Trimble's house and found him having his dinner. The dwarf threw the boy a crust dipped in gravy and told him that as soon he had finished eating there were some more errands to do.

"I'm going to have my after-dinner nap," he said, lying down on a sofa. "Wake me when you've finished cleaning up."

William was too excited even to eat his crust. As soon as he heard Trimble snoring loudly William slipped the magic pebbles into the slippers. They came off as easily as could be, and in great delight he ran over to Trimble. As soon as the slippers were off, William began to count.

"One–two–three," he counted, as he began to slip the shoes on to Trimble's feet – but to his horror the dwarf's feet were far too large – twice the size of William's! Whatever could he do?

"Four, five, six, seven, eight, nine—" he continued to count in despair, for the shoes certainly would *not* go on the dwarf's feet. And then, at the very last moment William had an idea. He would put them on the dwarf's hands!

He fitted them on quickly, counting "Ten!" as he did so – and at the same moment the dwarf awoke!

"What are you doing?" he cried angrily, jumping up. "I'll turn you into a frog, I'll—"

"Walk to the moon!" shouted William, in excitement – and then a most extraordinary thing happened! For the dwarf suddenly stood on his hands and began to walk on them out of his cottage! Trimble was even more astonished than William.

"Mercy! Mercy!" he cried. "Take these slippers off."

"I don't know how to," said William. "But anyway, it serves you right. Go on, slippers – walk to the moon and then, if the dwarf has repented of his bad ways, you may bring him back again!"

The dwarf was soon a long way off, walking upside down on his hands, weeping and wailing.

As soon as the dwarf was out of sight a crowd of little folk came running up to William. They were dressed in red and green tunics and had bright happy faces.

"We are the hill-brownies," they said, "and we've come to thank you for punishing that horrible dwarf. Now we shall all be happy, and you and your friends can walk safely up the hillside. Ho ho! Wasn't it a surprise for Trimble to be sent walking to the moon on his hands! That was very clever of you."

The jolly little hill-brownies took William safely back home, and even fetched his lost boots for him out of the bog into which they had sunk. And now William and his friends walk unafraid all over the hills, for the friendly brownies are about now and the nasty dwarfs have fled, frightened by the fate of Trimble.

As for Trimble he hasn't even walked halfway to the moon yet, so goodness knows when he'll be back!

3

Jumbo Saves
the Day

Illustrated by Maggie Downer

Outside the playroom window, inside an old flower-pot, lived three small pixies called Briar, Berry and Buttercup. The toys knew them very well indeed, for the pixies often came into the playroom at night when it was dark, and played with them.

Briar and Berry were big strong pixies, but Buttercup was small and sweet. She was their sister, and they loved her very much. All the toys loved her too, and they let her ride in the wooden train, and the toy motor car, and even on the big rocking-horse as many times as she liked.

Buttercup liked all the toys except big Jumbo, the grey elephant. He had once trodden on her toe by accident, and now she was frightened of him. Jumbo was sad about this, because he liked Buttercup very much, and was always longing to give her a ride on his back. But she never would ride on him, for he was too big and clumsy.

The toys belonged to two children called Amy and Andrew, but lately the children hadn't bothered to play with their toys very often. Their Uncle Jim had given them something they liked much better – two pairs of roller skates! You should have seen how the two children tore round and round on them! Goodness, they went like lightning!

The toys were jealous of the roller skates. The children kept them in the toy cupboard but every night the toys pushed them out.

"They are nasty things," said the clockwork clown, giving the skates a push. "I don't know why the children like them better than they like us. Get out of the toy cupboard, you ugly things! You don't belong in here!"

Then, bump-bump! Out would tumble the four skates on to the floor. They weren't alive, so they didn't mind one way or another. But the children were always puzzled to know how it was their skates fell out of the toy cupboard so often!

So every night the toys were very glad when the three pixies came to join them.

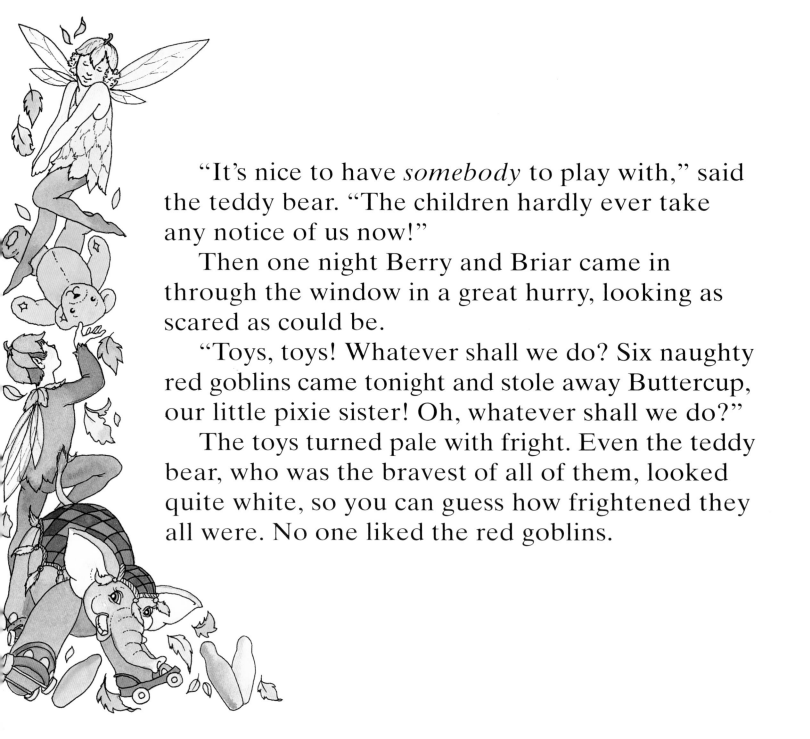

"It's nice to have *somebody* to play with," said the teddy bear. "The children hardly ever take any notice of us now!"

Then one night Berry and Briar came in through the window in a great hurry, looking as scared as could be.

"Toys, toys! Whatever shall we do? Six naughty red goblins came tonight and stole away Buttercup, our little pixie sister! Oh, whatever shall we do?"

The toys turned pale with fright. Even the teddy bear, who was the bravest of all of them, looked quite white, so you can guess how frightened they all were. No one liked the red goblins.

They were very naughty and liked nothing better than to play nasty tricks on people. They had once poured glue all over the playroom window-sill in the hope that one of the toys would get stuck there. Another time they had stolen pieces from all the children's jigsaws so that none could be finished completely. And now they had taken away Buttercup! Whatever could be done?

"They'll have taken her back to Goblin Land!" said the panda. "That's a long way from here!"

"Well, you can't ask *me* to go after them," said the clockwork train, in a hurry. "I can only run on my rails."

"And my key is lost," said the clockwork motor car. "*I* can't go!"

"Nobody wants to go!" wailed the two pixies sorrowfully. "Poor Buttercup! She'll never come back again." Then the big elephant, Jumbo, spoke up in his big deep voice.

"*I* will go and chase those goblins!" he said. "I'm not afraid!"

"Dear old Jumbo!" cried all the toys together. "What a kind, brave elephant you are! But you're so slow and clumsy it would take you ages to get there."

"Ah, but I've got a splendid idea!" said Jumbo. "I want you to strap those roller skates on to my big feet. Then, if you'll help me to practise, I shall go like the wind, roller-skating down the paths to Goblin Land!"

Well, what an idea! Did you ever hear anything like it! An elephant on roller skates! Anyway, you should have seen how the toys and the two pixies clapped their hands when they heard what Jumbo said. They thought it was the best idea they had ever heard.

"Quick! Get the roller skates!" cried Berry.
"Where are they?" cried Briar.
Panda got one, Teddy found another, and the two biggest dolls brought the last two.

Then they strapped them on to Jumbo's big, clumsy feet. He *did* look funny!

"I'm just going to have a skate round the playroom to see if I can do it properly," said Jumbo, shaking with excitement. And off he went, round and round the room.

Crash! Crash! Crash! went his feet, as he tried his hardest to skate with all four at once. Dear me, you should have seen him!

All the toys got out of his way in a great hurry, for his four feet shot out all over the place, and he didn't know at all where he was going. He knocked the clockwork clown flat on his nose and ran over the teddy bear's big toe. Goodness, it was a sight to see!

"Steady on, Jumbo!" called Berry, jumping up on to a chair for safety. But as soon as he sat down, Jumbo bounced into the chair and sent it flying! Down fell poor Berry with a crash. Up he got and climbed up on to the window-sill, feeling certain that Jumbo couldn't knock *that* down!

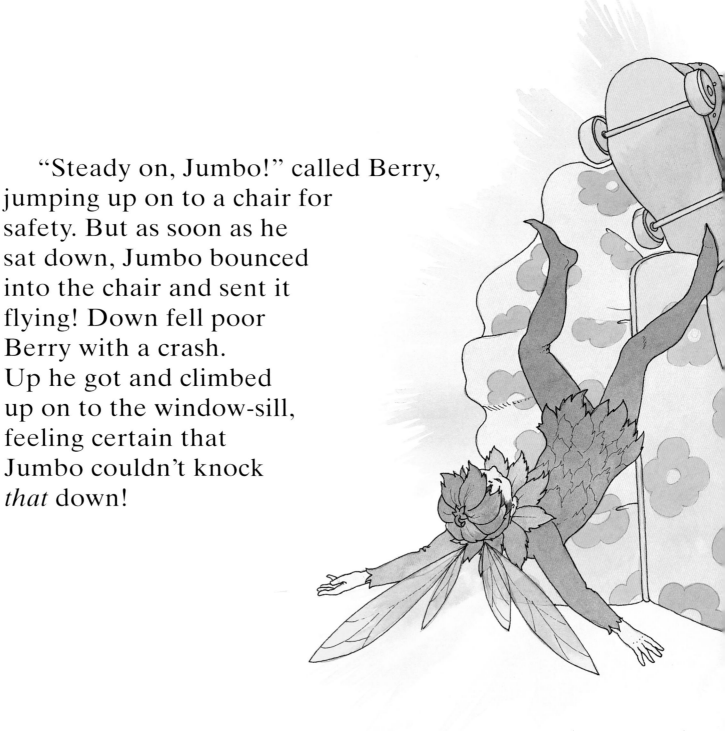

After a little while Jumbo began to skate much better. His legs went properly and he found that he could skate right round the nursery and back again without falling over once. He did feel proud.

"Now I'm ready to go after Buttercup and the goblins," he said to the pixies. "Jump up on my back and tell me the right way to go."

So Berry and Briar jumped up on to his broad back, and hung on tightly. Crash! Crash! Crash! went the roller skates as Jumbo skated out of the room and down the passage that led to the garden. What a noise he made! It's a wonder he didn't wake the whole house up!

Berry and Briar soon managed
to unlock the back door and
the three of them slipped
out into the garden.
The moon was shining
brightly as Jumbo went
skating splendidly
down the garden
path.

If one of his feet slipped he still had three others to help him, so he didn't fall over at all.

He *did* go at a rate! Out into the lane he skated and over the hill, until he came to the extra-large rabbit-hole that was the entrance to Goblin Land.

The streets of Goblin Land are very straight and smooth, so soon Jumbo found he could go even faster! Crash! Crash! Crash! went his skates and he tore along faster than any motor car could possibly go. Berry and Briar soon lost their hats, for the wind streamed past them and snatched away their hats with greedy fingers.

"There they are, there they are!" shouted Berry suddenly, so loudly that he frightened Briar and nearly made him fall off Jumbo's back. Jumbo looked in front of him and saw, far in the distance, a crowd of little red goblins riding yellow rocking-horses. One of them held Buttercup tightly in his arms, whilst he shouted to his rocking-horse to rock faster and faster through Goblin Land.

Jumbo made a sound like a trumpet and skated on faster than ever. The goblins heard the crash of his skates and looked back. When they saw Jumbo roller-skating behind them, carrying Berry and Briar on his back, they could hardly believe their eyes. They shouted loudly to their rocking-horses.

"Go on! Go on! You must go faster still! Hurry, hurry, hurry!"

The rocking-horses rocked away till it seemed as if they must tumble on their noses or tails. They went very fast indeed. But Jumbo went even faster. How he skated! You could hardly see his legs moving, they went so quickly.

"They're taking Buttercup to the Deep Green Cave!" cried Berry suddenly. "Oh dear, catch them before they get there, Jumbo, or we shall never see our dear little sister again!"

Sure enough,
they were heading
straight for the Deep
Green Cave, the place
where all the goblins'
nastiest magic is made. Jumbo
skated even faster to get there
before the goblins did – and he got
there with just a single second to spare.

Now luckily, Jumbo was so big that he easily blocked the entrance to the Deep Green Cave. And as the first goblin came rocking towards him, Jumbo scooped him up in his big long trunk and left him dangling in the branches of a nearby tree.

He did the same with the second, and the third goblin, and the other three were so frightened by the big, brave elephant that they soon started rocking in the opposite direction. But not before Jumbo had gently rescued Buttercup, of course! "On my back, quick, all of you!" shouted Jumbo, in his trumpeting voice, for he was sure that the red goblins would soon be back with some nasty magic to help them.

Berry jumped up. Then it was Buttercup's turn. She had quite forgotten that she had said she never, ever would ride on Jumbo's back so she got up as quickly as ever she could, and Briar followed close behind her.

Then back went Jumbo through Goblin Land, skating as fast as his four legs would carry him. Long before the red goblins came running after them, Jumbo was out of sight, crash-crash-crashing along on his four roller skates! It didn't take him long to get back to the playroom, very much out of breath, but simply delighted that Buttercup was safely home again. The toys gave him a great welcome, and cheered him with all their might. His trunk blushed quite red with pride.

The toys unstrapped the skates from his tired feet and put them away again. Then they heard the first cock crowing to say that day was coming, so they hurriedly said goodbye to the pixies and climbed back into the toy cupboard to go to sleep.

Berry and Briar patted Jumbo before they went, but Buttercup flung her arms round his trunk and kissed him lovingly.

"You're a dear, brave Jumbo," she said, "and I'm sorry I ever said you were clumsy. I'll come and ride on you every single night if you'll let me!"

Then off she went, and left Jumbo standing by himself, very happy indeed. And he was happier still the night after, for Buttercup came back and kept her promise. Good old Jumbo carried her all around the nursery and she wasn't frightened at all, no, not even for a minute!